MR. LAZY

by Roger Hargreaves

PSS!
PRICE STERN SLOAN

Mr. Lazy lives in Sleepyland, which is a very lazy-looking and sleepylike place.

The birds in Sleepyland fly so slowly they sometimes fall out of the sky.

The grass takes so long to grow that it only needs cutting once a year.

Even the trees are lazylooking and sleepylike.

And do you know what time everybody gets up in Sleepyland?

The answer is, they don't get up in the morning.

They get up in the afternoon!

Anyway, this story starts with Mr. Lazy being fast asleep in bed. In Sleepyland they call that being slow asleep!

He spends rather a lot of time in bed. It's his favorite place to be!

He opened his eyes, yawned, yawned again—and went back to sleep.

Later, Mr. Lazy opened his eyes again, yawned, yawned again, and went back to sleep again.

Much later, Mr. Lazy got up and went to make his breakfast.

We say breakfast, although really it was lunchtime.

He put the kettle on to make some tea. Kettles take two hours to boil in Sleepyland!

Then he toasted a slice of bread. Bread takes three hours to toast in Sleepyland!

Toast never gets burnt there!

While he was waiting for his kettle to boil and his bread to toast, Mr. Lazy went into the garden of Yawn Cottage—which was were he lived.

He sat on a chair. And you can probably guess what happened next.

That's right. He yawned, and yawned again, and went to sleep.

Suddenly he woke up with a jump, which is something that doesn't happen very often to Mr. Lazy.

And the reason he woke up with a jump was because of the noise.

"WAKE UP," said the noise.

"WAKEUPWAKEUPWAKEUP."

There were two men standing in front of him.

"I'm Mr. Busy," said one of the men.

"And I'm Mr. Bustle," said the other.

"Come along now," said Mr. Bustle busily.

"We can't have you sleeping all day," added Mr. Busy, bustling Mr. Lazy to his feet.

"But who are you?" asked Mr. Lazy.

"We're Bustle and Busy," they replied.

"Oh," said Mr. Lazy.

"Come along now," said Mr. Busy, "we haven't got all day."

"But...," said Mr. Lazy.

"No time for buts," said Mr. Busy. "Or ifs," added Mr. Bustle.

"There's the wood to chop and the beds to make and the floors to clean and the coal to get and the windows to polish and the plates to wash and the furniture to dust and the grass to cut and the hedges to clip and the food to cook!"

"And the clothes to mend," added Mr. Busy.

"Oh, dear," groaned Mr. Lazy in a daze. "The wood to clean and the beds to get and the floors to cut and the coal to cook and the windows to make and the plates to mend and the furniture to chop and the grass to wash and the hedges to dust and the clothes to clip?"

He'd got it all completely wrong he was in such a daze.

Then Bustle and Busy set Mr. Lazy to work.

Chopping and making and cleaning and getting and polishing and washing and dusting and cutting and clipping and cooking and mending.

Not to mention all the fetching and carrying!

Poor Mr. Lazy!

"Now," they said when he'd finished, "it's time for a walk!"

And off they set on the longest walk Mr. Lazy had ever been on.

Mr. Lazy is one of those people who never walks when he has a chance of sitting down, and never sits down when he has a chance of lying down.

But this day he had no choice. They made him walk for miles and miles and miles, until he felt his legs must be worn right down to his body.

Poor Mr. Lazy!

When they arrived back at Yawn Cottage, Mr. Busy said, "Right! Now for a run!"

"Oh, no," groaned Mr. Lazy.

"When I blow this whistle," said Mr. Bustle producing a whistle, "you've got to start running."

"As fast as you can," added Busy.

Mr. Lazy groaned a deep groan, and closed his eyes.

Mr. Bustle put the whistle to his lips.

"Wheeeeeeeeeeeeee," whistled the whistle.

"Wheeeeeeeeeeeeeee," went the whistle.

Mr. Lazy, poor Mr. Lazy, started to run.

But his legs weren't getting him anywhere.

He opened his eyes and looked down to see why.

And the reason his legs weren't getting him anywhere, was because he was sitting on a chair in the garden.

And there was no sign of Mr. Busy and Mr. Bustle!

It had all been a terrible dream!

And the whistle was the whistling kettle boiling in the kitchen!

Mr. Lazy heaved a sigh of relief.

And then he went into the kitchen, and sat down to have his breakfast, and to think about his dream.

But you know what happened next, don't you?

"Wake up, Mr. Lazy!"

"WAKEUPWAKEUPWAKEUP!"